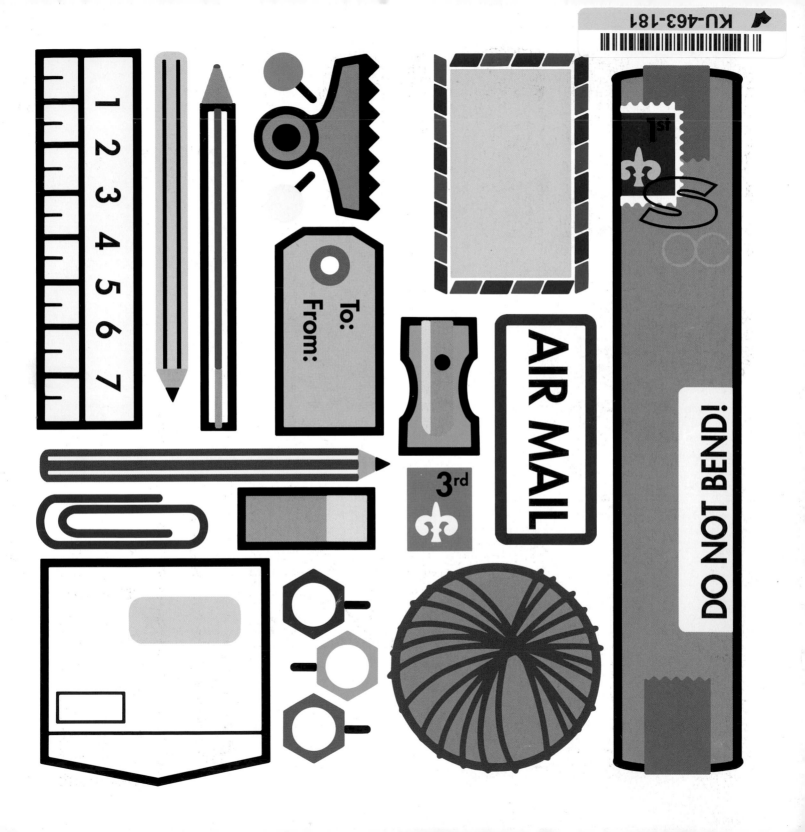

JONATHAN CAPE

UK | USA | Canada | Ireland | Australia
India | New Zealand | South Africa

Jonathan Cape is part of the Penguin Random House group of companies
whose addresses can be found at global.penguinrandomhouse.com.

www.penguin.co.uk   www.puffin.co.uk   www.ladybird.co.uk

Penguin
Random House
UK

First published in Great Britain 2019
001

Printed in China
A CIP catalogue record for this book is available from the British Library

ISBN: 978–1–780–08051–2

All correspondence to:
Jonathan Cape, Penguin Random House Children's
80 Strand, London WC2R 0RL

MIX
Paper from
responsible sources
FSC® C018179

williambee
Stanley
the Postman

JONATHAN CAPE • LONDON

It's still dark outside, but the lights are on in Stanley's Post Office.

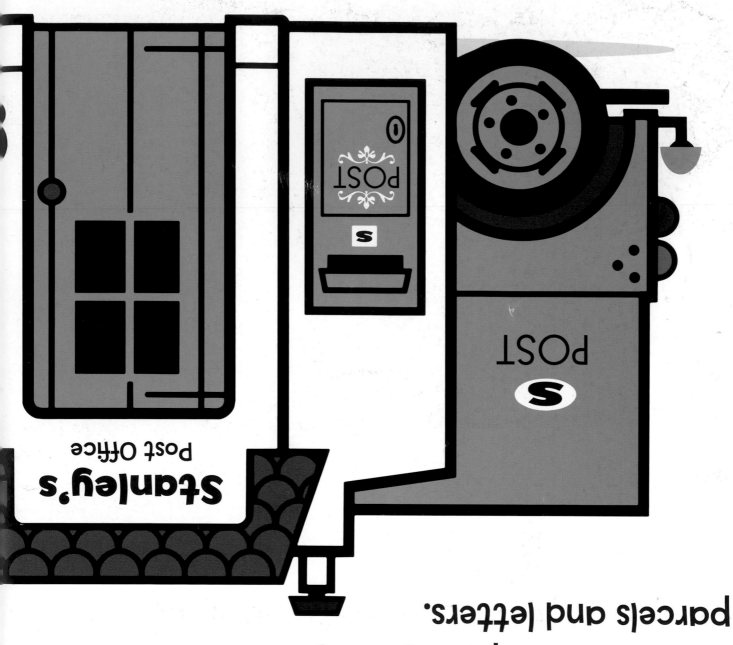

Stanley gets up very early to sort all the parcels and letters.

Then he sets off on his scooter –
everyone will be waiting for their post!

First stop - Myrtle's house.
Myrtle is delighted - it's something she ordered
from her favourite fancy shop in Paris!

What a lovely big box!
What a lot of tissue!

What a tiny little hat.

Next Stanley stops at Shamus and
Little Woo's house. It's a present for
Little Woo - he's very excited!

To Little Woo,
Shamus and Little Woo's
House, just down the road
from Myrtle's House,
before you get to
Charlie's House.

It's from Grandma and Grandpa,
and has come all the way from their house.

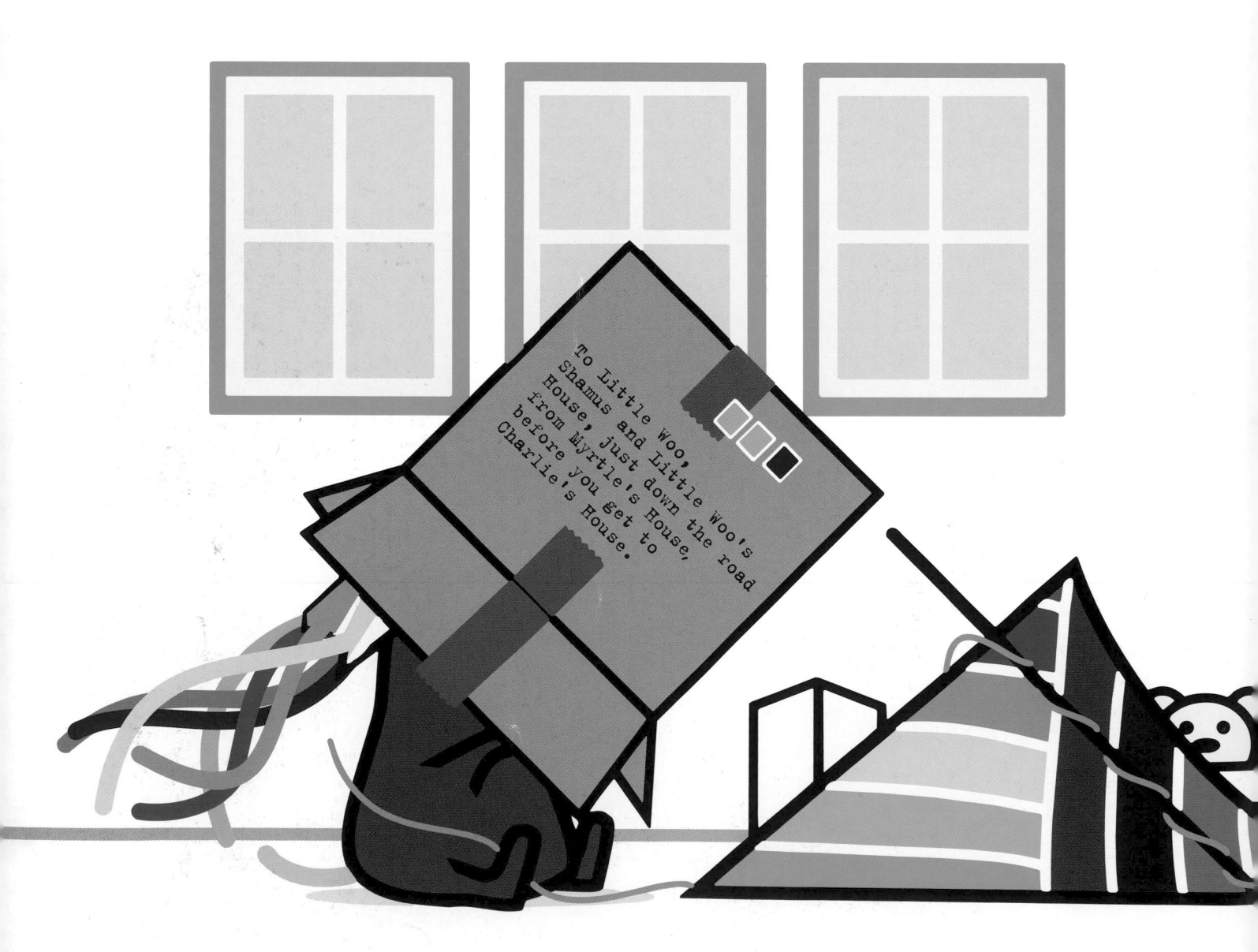

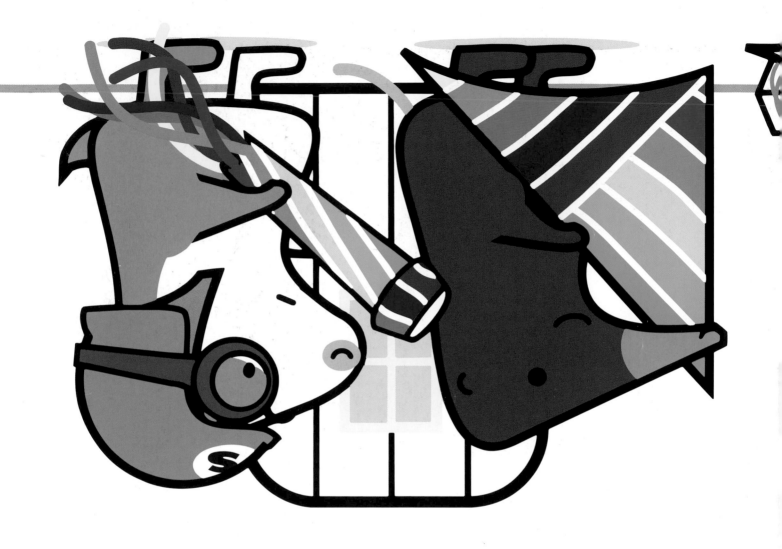

But what is it?
Luckily Little Woo's dad knows.

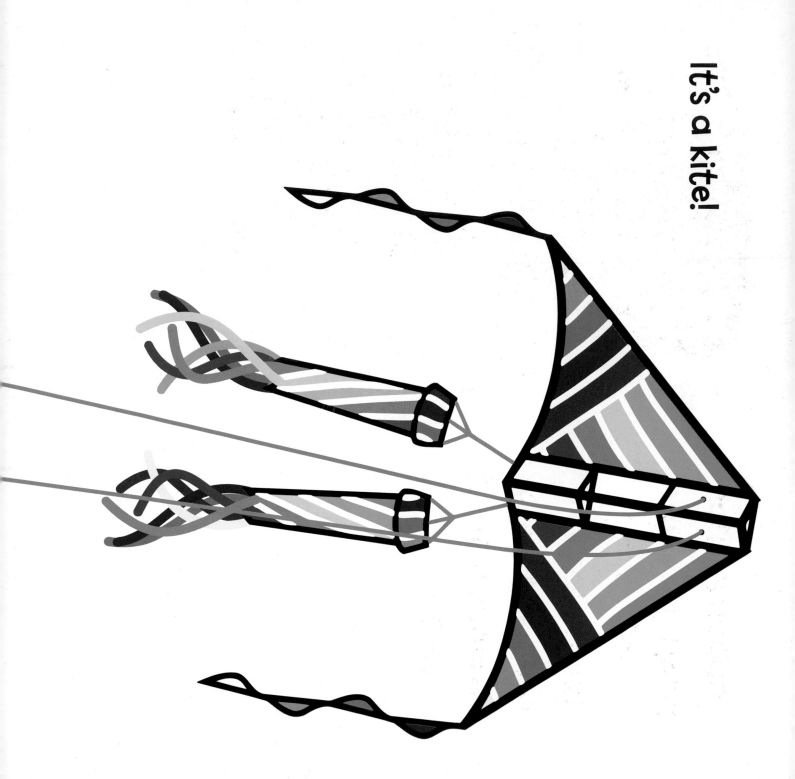

It's a kite!

The biggest, most wonderful kite Little Woo has ever seen! Thank you, Grandma! Thank you, Grandpa!

On to Charlie's house. Charlie has so much post that Stanley has gone back to the post office to get his post van.

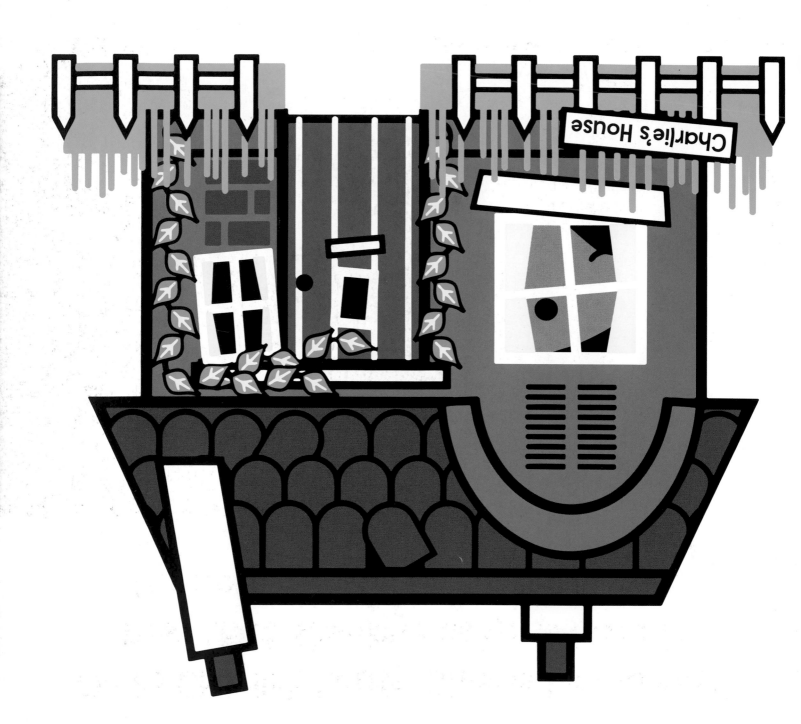

Charlie gets a lot of love letters –

he's quite a catch!

But not everyone is happy with what they got in the post - Hattie has another speeding ticket.
Well . . . THANK YOU, Stanley!

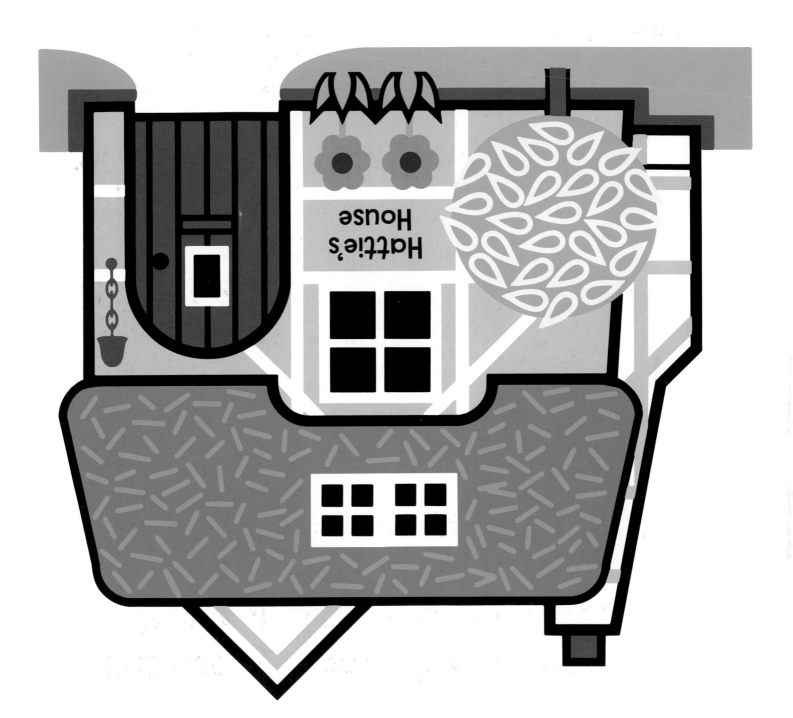

Well! What a busy day!

Stanley's Back Door

Time for tea!
Time for a bath!

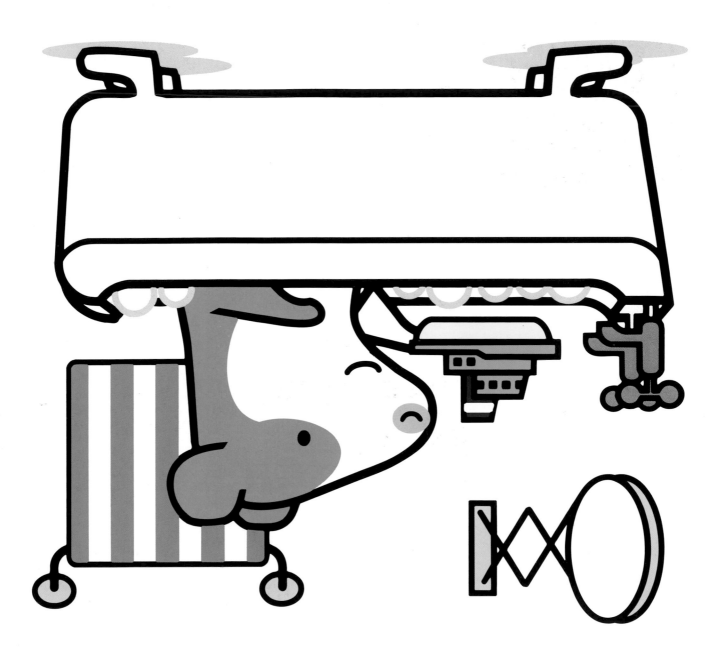

And time for bed!
Goodnight, Stanley.

Stanley

If you liked **Stanley the Postman** then you'll
love these other books about Stanley:

Stanley the Builder

Stanley's Café

Stanley the Farmer

Stanley's Garage

Stanley's Shop

Stanley's School

Stanley's Numbers

Stanley's Opposites

Stanley's Colours

Stanley's Shapes